CW01095863

Wonder and the Medicine Wheels

A Rainbow Warrior's Tale

A Story by Pàl Ó' Siadhail

Wonder and the Medicine Wheels
Pàl Ó' Siadhail

eBook Edition First Published in the United Kingdom in 2018
Paperback First Published in the United Kingdom in 2018

ISBN: 978-1-910757-44-4
aSys Publishing 2018

www.wonderandthemedicinewheels.com

Do Dhùghall agus do Fhionnghal mo chridh'

A time will come when the earth and all of life will need our help. At this time, a tribe will gather from all cultures of the world. They will be recognized by their spirit connection and life-giving action towards the finned, the winged, the creepy crawling, the standing green growing, the four legged and two legged nations, and all that is. They will awaken humankind to find a star within themselves. This star will guide them to overcome the mountains of ignorance, prejudice, hatred and fear through compassion, harmony, and honour. They will find a new song and a new dream. We are living in this time now. All of us with this vision are the tribe, we are the rainbow warriors, we will heal the world. We are the cherished vision and dream of the ancient ones of long ago.

—Blackfoot, Silversong Cree

Contents

To the Reader

Did once take flight on light wings,
the breath that catches freedom's sigh,
hurled by imagination's pearls
of sunbeams dark and lonely?

Did once ever cry a thousand dreams,
that enraged the tempest's flitting,
a wrathful mouth of love unchained,
lost in heaven's shadow?

Did once bend the harp of mountainous floods,
that poured sweet thoughts in flowing?
Did ever grieve misery that clung to walls,
a-scratching for fruitful forests?

Then what became of the dance of flowers,
a-plunder 'neath fiery rainfall?
Did yield ever youth to burden's sorrow,
choking in a healing of blindness?

For who is he that swiftly scribes,
in tongues of strange beguiling,
an empty stroke of spirit wind
a-begging for rugged beauty?

Did not part the oceans to honour the bee,
seeking of fruit and playful rhymes?
Where destiny smirks a knowing of paths,
that would shake the Devil's quaking.

Once lit eyes that equalled the sun,
a carving of clefts for ancient voyage,
a thundering of truth, a smelting of dreams,
silent yet full of loudness.

Shalt thou not come to the broken village,
where lies in vigour a smouldering fire,
where stories told can pull traveller's hearts,
deep in mighty snowfall?

Wonder and the Medicine Wheels

Has already been sensed, the warmth,
of the yonder glow of her spiralling embers,
that reddens the sunless vacuum of poets,
seeking the key to the immaculate doorway?

For exists there beyond the threshold,
the bright hurricane of the soul,
that sharply blasts all shaping and moulding,
the mystique of the lonely wayfarer.

What learned he, the sad voyager,
but of the howling of fierce crosswinds,
unravelling the secret of the powerful oak tree,
all forged in a gnarled beauty of awe.

Dost thou hear the bleeding on the wind
of the unfathomable lullaby,
that loudly calls amidst the emptiness,
of the unmeaningful blabber of tongues?

Is forgotten the intelligence
of the raven of watchful nests,
ever pondering and questioning,
in his flight of worldly conversation?

For hear but the creaking of frozen lakes,
awaiting to crack and quench
the desert's scorching.

For is not suppression but emotion,
springily trapped?
Silent is the rumbling
of the waning of direction.

Is not the winter's basking,
of cruelty and mourning,
but the revealer of dreams
of the endless days?

Doth the summer's repose,
echo of tales,
of spines without their vigour?

Doth thou scent of the table
where apathy dines,
a-toasting to masters shallow?

Where poison lurks in hidden coil,
sparkling of gold and gemstones.

Wonder and the Medicine Wheels

Didst thou ever hear the voice
that once shook the high peaks?
Didst thou ever contemplate
the song of the stream?

Didst thou ever give taste
to the fragrance of snowdrops?
Didst thou ever escape
the swiftness of dreams?

Long ago when the valleys were young
came blood a-reaping his twisted harvest,
a gnawing of spirit and kindly eyes,
that would shame the sky's vast kingdom.

Darkness gave witness
to the flood of battleships,
concealing many tombstones
was the cluster of flame,

dipped in blindness,
bellowed a rage all trembling,
sharp were the horns that blasted the sands.

Shuddering were the footsteps
of the king of magic,
long was his shadow,
that cast on an ancient shore.

Quivering were the hearts
of the simple people,
asleep in trust and meekness.

As the grandeur of ritual
smothered the stars,
was not Wonder awake in his wisdom?

For long had he starved
of love and sunbeams,
fleeing from the cruel and mocking.

Can love be born in anger's bosom?
Can rage come forth in simple manner?

Though I know not all
the many ways of the hurricane,
I cannot say but that I know of its blast!

Is it not the keeper who unhinges the latch?
Is not Time but the watcher,
all creeping and restless?

Is it lost or heartfelt, openings lonely?
Doth crystal waters give life to the well?

Was once ever felt the thrust
of the point of the snowstorm,
cold, not numb, of perceptions presence?

Were once ever torn the leaves
from prophecy's grasp,
discarding the serpent's trickery?

And so unto thee
a conscience in rambling,
doth the sand maketh the mountain?
Or doth the mountain dwell in the sand?

Doth the tuneful robin bend
to the great north wind?
Doth the lasting pine tree,
know of his shadow?

Is it wide eyed and narrow,
the dream in thine eye?
Is it pain that has abashed,
the petals countenance?

Let not lies and rasping sneers,
cut of the flesh,
let the music of the firmament
give breath to the rock,
until she stands on firm ground.

Has broken the heart,
that gave his love to the long grass?
Has stalled the mill,
of the turning of softness?

Has ignorance bred a fertile plain,
that growls at the daylight's shyness?

Yet still blots the leaf
a swishing of symbols,
born of the ether in curious sound,

perhaps a land of the imagination in motion,
where empathy soars with eagle's sense.

A goading of rainbows,
all blinding and flashing,
was it not the Creator's hand,
that gave life to the flint?

Has rusted the mighty anvil,
the blacksmith's brother,
is without meaning, the sucking,
of the hammer's wind?

Is burdensome the rainfall,
endless and not waning?
Confusion is diligent,
a weight of seven oceans.

Has forgotten the darkness,
the fruits of dawn,
shapeless in his vastness,
not mindful of promise?

Did yield tender kindness
to the absence of song?
Was she rigid in flowing
the cackle of geese?

Is it not of the tempest,
a disturbing of dust?
Is it not sightless, the road,
of the hunter of courage?

Long and narrow
are the tunnels of old,
frightful is their trail
ground of lostness and feeling.

Wonder and the Medicine Wheels

Yet bright is the lute
of the maiden of dreams,
doth thine eyes not weep
to the glistening of stars?

Seen I have,
a many twisting of paths,
skilled are the hands
that guide and mould.

Wide is the horizon,
where ponders and swirls, the artist,
thirsty is the broken cup of denial,
consumed by many untruths.

For where is it she resteth,
The Well of Omens,
loving of the long grass
and the kingdom of birds?...

Introduction

So the day came to pass
when the great rolling sun
cast his mournful rays for the last time
on The Kingdom of the Crystal Lake.

The mountainous land
where the eagle of lofty heights,
spreads her wings,
bending to the call of freedom.

The rugged land of the breathing pine tree,
where the forgotten oak graces the forest,
smiling with secrets of a bygone age.

The land of the leaping salmon and silver rivers,
where great lakes lie in their ancient majesty,
whispering potent charms of the old ways.

A land flowing of milk and tasteful honey,
where the golden corn leans in friendship
to the great north wind,
that fills the heart with a clean air,
pure like the tumbling waterfall
cascading its way into vastness.

"No more will ears hear the sound
of the cuckoo in his leafy den!"
cried the pine marten to the chirping red robin,
lamenting to the song
which bore the world into being,
bearing her fruitful offerings.

"What of me?" gnarled the nimble mountain lion,
beholding of the bounty of the sheltering forest,
roaming to the strange guidance
of Earth Mother's silent drum.

"And I too, what shall become of me?"
snarled the howling white wolf,
shining in his coat of a hundred thousand winters.

For bustling was the great forest
that fateful night
when the red rolling sun bid farewell
to The Kingdom of the Crystal Lake.

"Many questions ye have!"
bellowed the aged soothsayer
unto all the animals,
gleaming with his white beard
that danced with the heavenly moonbeams.

13

Pàl Ó' Siadhail

"Come has the frightful age
of the Relentless Snow Blast,
where reigns the Devil on his icy throne,
lost in his darkness
without care or without love for Earth Mother."

"Then fight we must!"
snorted the boar of sharp tusks
from his blissful boggy abode.

"Ye know as well as I,
that since the Great Salmon of Omens
appeared in the starry realms
many harvests ago above the sea of clouds,
that fought bravely we have
to protect Earth Mother,"

replied the wise soothsayer.

"To live and fight another day we must,
O dear wild creatures of the rough bounds!"

"Be mindful of prophecy,"

rutted the king of stags,

"For the Great Spirit that dwells
in every living thing,
asks for us to be his keepers,
for shall come again the time
when all living creatures
shall listen to the forgotten tales of the golden age
in the fabled Kingdom of the Crystal Lake."

"Wise is he that speaks of prophecy,"
hooted old grandmother owl of the tree tops,
full of sight and hunting,

"For already has been born the song
of the Rainbow Warrior
in the great starry kingdom
above the sea of clouds.

Take to our hiding we must,
O heartbroken brothers and sisters.
Earth Mother lies in her waiting
full of beauty and awe for her wandering children,
for shall come again the time
when the great wisdom shall lend his whistle
to the tameless breeze,
and up to us it is here this night,
to keep alight the flame of the bright knowledge!"

Then did play the dreaming piper,
the ancient pipes,
with a bittersweet melody,
so to move all living things unto a tearful joy,
to which clung the lamenting poet
in his crossed stitched cloth
full of verse and kindness.

"Tear the heart that bellows from out my breast,
spill forth a thousand rivers red and twisting,
nourish the land of the leafy willow,
bend to the grief of mournful song,
O forgotten children of the lofty pine trees.

Where is it thou sleepest?
Doth the heather make a bed for thee,
whispering in thine ear of beauty and daydreams?
Shalt thou not lift thy head softly and caring,
and awaken from the dormancy
of thy visionless soul,
O children of the land of milk and corn?

Land of oats, abounding in fruit,
where the unflagging little mouse
scratches his thoroughfare,
baffling the cunning of the skipping fox,
ever hungry in his search for nourishment.

"Art thou awake yet with sleepy eyes
full of forgetfulness?
Or does the rambling of tongues numb thy wits?

Has the scent of bluebells
carried thee away unto a distant shore,
where the silent piper enchants the wind,
rustling the corn with sound of song
from a bygone age?

Pàl Ó' Siadhail

Canst thou feel the earth
beneath thine ancient feet,
O children of the mountain passes,
graceful like the eagle of high heights,
soaring over the mountain tops with sharp wings?
Doth thine ears hear the voice of old
that thunders amidst the valleys
bountiful with grass and shrubs?
Do they hearken unto the rumble
of the distant trampling of footsteps,
which beckon the enticement
to the calling of adventure?

"Dost thou hear?...
Canst thou hear?...
Shalt thou hear?..."

Chapter 1

Summary

While out walking one day in the Ancient Forest of
Pathfinders, Wonder hears a mysterious voice calling
on the wind singing to him about a mysterious journey.
With fear and uncertainty in his heart, he decides to
follow the voice to see if he can locate her whereabouts.
He crosses beyond the forbidden boundary stone into
a world of legend and myth where the mysterious
song of the Rainbow Warrior has been preserved.
After much searching, Wonder eventually encounters
a beautiful mermaid basking in the moonlight at the
foot of a mighty waterfall that tumbles into a Crystal
Lake. The mermaid imparts to him a parable of the
teachings of Earth Mother and how she is again calling
for the rise of the Rainbow Warrior famed in legend.

Chapter 1

The Rousing of the Wayfarer

Pàl Ó' Siadhail

Come gather 'round children
of the wilderness and daydreams.
From the rugged land of the lofty pine,
to the great rolling and fertile plains.

Willst thou not lend an ear
to the sway of forgotten tongues?
A most puzzling of journeys,
many poets and travellers shall tell.

For this here tale is of adventure,
from a time long, long ago,
all about a pondering child called Wonder,
misty but potent legends recall,
that he once drank from a wishing well.

Deep and dreaming was his spirit,
from the moment he was born,
full of play was the child,
who lived for the sparkle of his mother's eyes,

which did dance in merriment like the rising sun,
of a sweet, sweet summer's morning,
for many are the ways that awaken the silent song
of the blessed gift of life.

Wonder and the Medicine Wheels

Now one day whilst out a-walking
through the Ancient Forest of Pathfinders,
where the Devil of legends told
the Enchanted Elves and Fairies hide,

on the ever-restless wind,
heard Wonder a strange voice,
lamenting of love and wisdom,
and the lost and hallowed art,
of the game called seek and find.

"For far away in thy heart
lieth a winding road,
that shall twist and turn,
leading far beyond the walls of thy mind.

Dear child, like sparrow hawk thou art,
but never shalt thou soar above the sharp peaks,
if the heart be deserted on the sacred earth,
feeling empty and left behind."

Pàl Ó' Siadhail

In amazement,
Wonder began eagerly searching
for the mysterious source
of the soothing voice,

for full of flight and mischief,
did tickle the butterflies within,
leaving Wonder numb of his wits,
without the ability of making choice.

Racing deeper and deeper
into the vastness of the ancient forest,
spellbound to the air
of the guiding and calming call,

when from far beyond in the distance,
emerged a most terrible thunder,
from the spewing mouth,
of a mighty and cascading waterfall.

Wonder and the Medicine Wheels

Bellowing louder and louder
with every light-some step,
the tempest bowed his head in shame,
for such was the force of the torrent's shake,

there rumbled forth a curious vision unto Wonder,
all whispering from the realms
of his second sight,
where he did gaze upon a mysterious land,
renowned far and wide,
as the fabled Kingdom of the Crystal Lake.

Lost in this strange perception,
all cold of his senses,
the boy crossed beyond
the forbidden boundary stone,
where lay a forgotten village of a peaceful people,
skilled in charms and lore,

where elders and chiefs
would sit around the fire in counsel,
reciting many epic stories and legends,
of giants of great deeds,
who walked the sacred mountains,
many icy winters before.

Pàl Ó' Siadhail

For not without verse nor scarcity of craft,
would pine songs of heroes
and path-finding braves,

where a Rainbow Warrior
would battle his shadow,
to free his heart and its secret ways.

For coiled in this sanctuary,
lies in hiding a gift,
a secret trail
full of questions and thought,

where the Rainbow Warrior
must clamber and toil,
to give breath to his dreams,
before they wither and rot.

***

With the sturdy green virgins
of the forest's domain,
now fading quickly from Wonder's sight,

his daydream crashed,
for the Earth Mother's ageless, swaying cycle,
had come calling for the night-time's somber veil,
to begin its smothering of the light.

But yonder soft sweet melody,
that clung to the wind that day,
did yet cry for the child's attention,

singing, "Between darkness and light,
is where all Rainbow Warriors
become masters of a strange invention!"

Hypnotized like a little field mouse
that had fallen prey
to the rocking motion
of a hunting snake's quiver,

Wonder now sensed
that the guiding lament,
led unto what he thought
was a great and trundling river.

For through the well wandered mist,
which wrestled with the sunset,
boundless was the mass of water
that could now be seen.

It was then Wonder's soul spoke
of the mystery of omens,
for before his eyes lay the crystal lake
that he had visioned in his daydream.

Looming grand mountains,
of the famed bounding deer's abode,
uncloaked their majesty
for the adventurer's keen eyes to see,

while all the animals sprightly stirred,
awakening the Fairies and Elves,
who cried passionately, "Alas!
Has arrived the days long foretold,
of the prophecy of the Rainbow Warrior,
rejoice O heartworn brothers and sisters,
has returned our time to roam and be free!"

From the deep sleep
of seven thousand winters,
weeping wails let sooth and mourn,

"Come gather every dream-tracker,
armed with sharp scythes,
give wind to the song of the harvest
of the golden corn."

Pàl Ó' Siadhail

A lagging of fog
revealed more of the fruitful magic,
the roaring waterfall reached
to the moon bold and high,

where she joined with the shimmer
of the twinkling stars,
many were the colours that blotted and swayed
across the ancient sky.

All the scrambling creatures
of the forest settled down,
nestling within the sacred yew tree's arms.

The king of stags conversed
with courageous badger and great bear,
while the intelligent fox boasted wildly
of his gifts of knowledge and charm.

Wonder and the Medicine Wheels

Then making his way
full of creeping in agile spine,
appeared the secretive nimble mountain lion,
who posed the question,
Where ye sit dost thou know of it's root?

Old grandmother owl of the tree tops,
replied in gliding tongue,
"After five hundred turns of the great rolling sun,
the yew tree withers, dies,
then bears fresh budding fruit!"

A group of giggling mice
applauded the battle of wisdom,
the chirping red robin gave breath
to his merry-making sound,

the howling white wolf with his coat
of a hundred thousand winters moaned,
the boar of sharp tusks, snorted happily,
from his blissful boggy ground.

Pàl Ó' Siadhail

Then, at the foot of the tumbling waterfall,
chasing a pair of mischievous otters,
a most peculiar creature swam among
the surging waves of bubbling foam,

before climbing onto a lonesome rock,
humming a peaceful lullaby,
which graced the air
causing the wind to stop and notice,
from his ever wandering, ceaseless, roam.

For before Wonder's eyes,
brimming with excitement and confusion,
was a beautiful mermaid basking in the glitter,
of a dripping silver moon,

a confirmation of legends,
old like the unseen growing of mountains,
the child's heart did thump loudly,
letting out a beating unearthly boom,

like the sound of a swarming army
full of piercing drums,
where truth and love stand on firm ground,
despite the Devil's gnashing fright,

hammering firmly their deep rhythms,
of defiance and bravery,
beckoning the blind seeker to enter,
beyond the gateway of chance and sight.

"What could be the meaning,
of this here mystery before me?"
thought pounced in his pondering,
consuming the child's mind.

"Is this here the maiden,
whose voice melts with the wind,
crying heartfully of adventure,
and the game called seek and find?"

Pàl Ó' Siadhail

A croaking of disturbance took flight
in the air above the sacred yew tree,
the black ravens,
whoever guarded the spirit world,
let crow their ghostly lay,

making way for aged Destiny,
who tirelessly shuffled along,
cloaked in his secrecy,
since the rising of the light of day.

The Devil – ever lurking – whispered terribly,
in his icy voice of fear,
truth and love clung to the moonbeams,
that turned dazzling the night time's sky.

Yonder beautiful mermaid, with green eyes,
and burning red hair,
cried a heart aching sorrow
where a cascade of tears,
gave life to her breath,
for her forgotten tongue, to fly.

"Feasgar math dhuit,
's math do choinneachadh a laochain,
's fhada a shiubhail thu an-diugh gu dearbh,
a sgrùdair bhig mo chridh',

tha mi air leth thoilichte gun tug thu sgrìob,
air seann rathad toinnte na coille,
chionn, tha e air a bhith corr is iomadh bhliadhna,
bhon a sheinn mi,
óran threòrachaidh nan sìtheachan!"

"Warm is the welcome unto thee,
O wandering child of many questions,
far and wide have you journeyed,
since the springing of the ballad of dawn,

narrow is the way which leadeth
unto the Kingdom of the Crystal Lake,
listen closely little pathfinder,
for has returned the time,
of the Rainbow Warrior and his forgotten song.

Pàl Ó' Siadhail

"Wonder, a most enchanted awakening
now stirs in the firmament,
an invisible shifting of consciousness,
unveiling truth for sleepy eyes,

from the heights of the sharp peaks,
to the green, leafy valleys,
where eagle's sense soars far beyond
the Devil's tricks and illusions,
and his gloomy world, of enticing lies.

For rekindled is Earth Mother's
smouldering fire,
loving is the breath that gives wind
to her flame that grows.

Of mystery is the hand
that tends to her embers,
which settle among the flickering stars
of the poet's sweet repose.

"Dearest child let me speak to thee,
of insight and questions,
that frequent midst the boundlessness
of the painter's quiet skill,

that draws from a lake,
gouged of bottomless crystal caverns,
where great depths of contemplation merge,
with the eddies never-ending swirl.

"Is it not love that steers the course
of the babbling brook,
that tumbles on its journey
toward distant land,

through gnarled canyons
all rushing and winding,
before learning of the ocean's vastness,
and her waves that crash upon the sand?

"Be then like the babbling brook,
that springs from her humble beginnings,
who knows of the ocean's greatness and strength,
that absorbs great tumbling force,

of torrents and floods and rivers that shake,
returning unto their oneness,
for the ocean's wholeness is not of separation,
but in eternal unity, with its trickling source.

"So verily I say unto thee,
O watchful child of the mountain passes,
let the tender heart surge in intuitive dreams,
spreading all wild and free,

for untamed is the stretching and countenance,
of the ancient oak tree,
who reflects in his stillness,
the mystery of what came to be!"

Chapter 2

Summary

Shocked at the truth of discovering a creature of myth and legend, Wonder's soul awakens and he begins to ponder the message that has been delivered to him by the beautiful mermaid. The mermaid asks him of his dreams and the nature of who he is, to which Wonder nervously tells her about his beloved Medicine Wheels and how along with his mix of music and rhymes he can raise the vibration of his people, helping them combat the dark controlling energy of the Devil. Recognizing the bliss that pours forth from Wonder when speaking of his bright dreams, the beautiful mermaid speaks to Wonder of the great strength that lies within him and if he is brave enough to follow his dreams that one day they will come true. Finally, the mermaid concludes with an offer of a challenge to Wonder to immerse himself in the mysterious waters of the Crystal Lake. Only by making this leap of faith into the unknown can Wonder continue on his road of discovery.

Chapter 2

The Birth of a Dream

Pàl Ó' Siadhail

So the legends recall that on this day,
such a long, long time ago,

a seed from the boy
burst forth into the horizon,
which would have to nimbly bend,
in order to grow.

Like the crooked oak tree
that shall twist with the wind,
and drink of the heavenly thunder,

dance with the sun
and chant with the snowstorms,
with the tight roots inside of Wonder.

That must grasp on with courage and grit,
so the seed may discover
the hidden secret in its form,

which quietly exists in the heart,
of every seeking dream-tracker,
a strange persistence like the breaking
of the morning ever born.

Wonder and the Medicine Wheels

For many changing seasons
not barren of trials must be braved,
for both the light and the darkness,
to nourish the seed,

for wisdom to blossom,
from the heart deep within,
where the toil of one's journey,
both laments and pines,
unto the forgotten power of creed.

For you see,
the beautiful mermaid asked of Wonder,
"Who art thou and what magic dost thou hold?

That shines from within thee,
thy soul and thy being,
what guardest thee from the Devil's wrath,
and his world of biting cold?"

Pàl Ó' Siadhail

Still wrapped in amazement
at this mythical creature,
Wonder again felt the churning
of the butterflies' wings inside,

which tickled his tongue
in bittersweet visions,
while his shyness prepared his unflown voice,
for his spirit dreams to glide….

"The Medicine Wheels!
The Medicine Wheels!
The weaving of music so soulfully spun,

from a golden thread of rhythm and rhyme,
a-beating earthily, from Earth Mother's drum.

"While the Horn of Echoes
giveth wings to my rhymes,
where the children of daydreams,
lose themselves to the essence,

caught in the crosswinds,
of the storyteller's hurricane,
full of the bright sunbeams,
of frantic poetry and cadence.

"A twisting breeze
of fragrant nectar and honey,
blowing forth the magic
of the dance of life,

where all the people smile
with freedom and love,
forgetting of the darkness,
and the trouble and strife.

"For the Devil and his artful trickery
has laid waste the land,
enslaving the children
and their dreaming ways,

while eyes have turned blind,
to the mystery within our souls,
lost in his pranks, his deceit,
and his lure-some gaze.

"So in many ways,
one may call me healer,
'midst the turmoil and rampant confusion,

for the poetry of the seeker
has cleared once muddied sight,
exposing not but a world
of subtle deception and illusion.

"Is not life's quest,
but to taste of love's deepness,
to spin with her threads
and her movement that flows?

"So that all may behold,
of her stitchwork and patterns,
and the sound of her silent piper,
that eternally blows."

The beautiful mermaid
then swiftly replied,
"Deep is the dream that breathes
its unborn cry,

a rumbling of visions
where the sharp hunter's grasp
is known to catch rainbows
and sapphire dew drops,
that not yet know how to fly!

"For great is the strength
that runneth within thee,
ceaseless is the wind
of the artist's mind,

that meanders and wanders,
not seeking of horizons,
but searching of laughter,
and his hidden treasure to find.

"But not without faith
nor void of will's strain,
can creation's force strangely bear fruit
to the bough of highest height,

ripe like the golden sun that creeps
over yonder misty mountain,
piercing the shadowy veil
at the bursting of the aurora,
to steal away the night.

"Not are these words
made of riddles to fool,
for old and wise are the roads
of the great unknown,

not scribed on calfskin
are the lost maps of the absolute,
which secrete in the imagination
of our innermost home.

"Be then like a mighty beacon,
loud and ablaze,
for many are the souls cast adrift
on the tortured sea of lies.

Let not ears fall deaf to ignorance,
nor let eyes turn blind to sadness,
let open the heart to the shuddering screams,
of the lonely traveller's cries!

Pàl Ó' Siadhail

"Then what became of the pilgrim
who followed the sun,
bereft and naked, but,
of the musical dance deep within,

who voyaged over land and sea,
acquiring many jewels of wisdom,
claiming wearily, yet passionately,
that the hardest part was to begin?

"For to gather the wind
of dreams' frightful beginnings,
comes not without the cutting
of a cruel tongue's sneer.

"Embrace the taunting and mockery
with wide open arms,
let love shine boldly, in all her beauty,
for no enemy has she, but fear.

"A tossing of emotions
shall run swiftly and heavy,
like the crashing of rivers,
that carve their form ground of rock,

the spirit, like water, carries within her,
the might of silver canyons,
chiselled of great intelligence and craft,
so peacefully and wildly wrought.

"Now Wonder child,
shalt thou choose to follow upon
the forgotten rainbow path of dreams,

thou must immerse thyself
in the mysterious waters of the Crystal Lake,
where revealed are her many invisible ways,
that are not ever, ever, as it seems!

Pàl Ó' Siadhail

"Lift thine untamed eyes
to the lofty mountain passes,
breath the deep learning,
of the leafy forest's treasure,

ponder in the grove
amidst the shade of rugged oak trees,
listen closely to the kingdom of birds,
content in their tuneful, chirping pleasure."

***

Like the wisp of joy
that bringeth love to the painter,
the revealer of worlds
that bears life to bright dreams,

did not Wonder then bravely leap
into the fabled waters of the Crystal Lake,
where lie many uncharted lands
of contemplation,
reflecting of thought,
and her torrents and streams.

A colliding of cold imagery
and gnashing of teeth,
did at once surround the child,
all terrible and frightful,

for the shadows that linger in the darkness
are known to bring gifts of sharp perception,
all full of hearing and listening,
but none the less, truly insightful.

Rapid and flashing
was the gushing of the current,
that carried Wonder far beyond
the threshold of ancient travellers,

where stories of old
tell of the mystery and magic,
of epic battles fought between
the Baffling Riddler
and the skill of the Great Unraveller.

And as the spirit of death came surging,
seeking of his capture,
did not boom an unseen voice
in philosophical song,
bringing tales of the unrelenting deep,

that bestowed the life of breath,
to the crushing of gasping lungs,
where the consciousness of the child
began slowly to return,
from the clutches of death,
who had come to reap...

Chapter 3

Summary

After jumping into the Crystal Lake and escaping the clutches of death, a mysterious voice begins to speak to Wonder, a voice of the spiritual philosophy of love, fear, bliss, heartache, joy, sadness, discovery, loneliness and of the ancient prophecy of the Rainbow Warrior.

Chapter 3

The Lost Mouth of the Crystal Lake

"Come, take my hand,
little dweller on the slipstream,
let go unto her mystic,
dear beloved traveller of the narrow path.

"Doth she not behold the scent
of the stillness of the gypsy's cry?
From where doth she spring,
the quiet voice that frequents the thin realms?

"Weary and confused is he
that grounds unmade trails,
far away from the solace
of the innocence of daydreams.

"Many are the staggering stories
that lie hidden amongst the fauna and flora,
each and every one perceived
of a most convincing truth.

"For is he not indeed humble,
the prince of fools,
who gazes into vastness?
Many are his questions,
bereft of understanding.

"Is weak the anger
that once enraged the burning sun?
Doth loneliness invade the bittersweet fervour
of a dying world in commotion?

"Dost thou wish to learn the ways,
of the torchbearer of the threshold?
Dost thou pine for the knowledge
of the dissolving of illusion?

"For to be of heaviness
is a strange load, dear child,
untamed by will and daydreams,

unyielding is the torment,
great is the power
of the deceiver and his presence!

Pàl Ó' Siadhail

"Is it blinding or for reason,
the occurring of trauma's seeping?
A slow thickening of blood
that curdles and clots.

"Doth the light exist
midst the darkness on tumbling shores?
Are not frightful the waves
that chisel rock to sand!

"Cool is the spirit,
the grace of the seasons,
doth not temper lie behind
the mask of a thousand faces?

"Unbeknown is the smile that hides
in the gloomy shafts and empty caves,
blackness exists there
in ceaseless icy droplets.

"Was not born the shining
of brightly eyes
that would fill the heavens
of the poet's sweet repose?

"Much is the pondering,
of the seeker in his distance,
not unburdened by great snowdrifts
is the plain of thought!

"From where was born the song
of the little birds,
abounding in the mirthfulness
of the endless chorus?

"Did the wind give life
to the whistler's need for air?
Are considered the mysteries,
that grace beyond the threshold?

Pàl Ó' Siadhail

"Is she concealed in her glowing,
the apparency of truth,
that rattles the keys
to the lonely drawbridge?

"Waiting is the doorway,
where the lost pilgrim travelled,
seen are the many voyages,
not beheld are the wakes and trails.

"Can love be moulded
by one's perception,
or doth she not require
the narrowness of minds?

"Doth confusion persist
like the dew of cold summers?
Of faith is the hunter
of the master bow!

"Why doth rage bubble upon
the stage of curious acts?
Is here felt the mirror
of the great reflector of deeds?

"Verily I say unto thee, little dream-tracker,
does the heart spill of love
or of the curse of jealousy?

"Is the duality of dimensions
yet cutting of swords?
Can peace be sprung
from anger and worthlessness?

"Can kindly eyes be found
in the heat of battle?
Doth not guide the torchbearer
through the teaching of meetings?

"Woe to the tongue
that sneers unwisely,
not of the ancient wisdom
is the loathing of breath.

"Shalt thou not turn
to the wind and cry,
for the desolate dweller
of mighty oceans?

"A shaper in his quest
of sense and virtue,
all tossed in calm and fury.

"Doth not the sun rise
on a mystic plain,
a consistent pattern
of curious order?

"Not without venom
is the serpent of gold and gemstones,
naked is the storyteller,
who reveals deep wounds and damaged story.

"Is stilled yet the voice
that pervades behind thick walls,
doth honesty and truth conceal themselves,
in far off distant mountains?

"Where at sometime or other,
all are drawn in the silence of loneliness,
what dwelleth there,
but the consuming ghost of righteousness,
the subtle evader of the untainted self!

"Was once ever glimpsed
the colour of the little flowers,
so beautiful in their countenance?

"Was she not heard,
the spellbinding sound
of the cuckoo of the abundant thicket?

Is felt the frost of the snowstorm,
that carries the load of the heaven's weight?

Does she bite all punishing,
the spirit world,
that surrounds the traveller in his desolation?

"But know this, O dream-tracker
of the stained stitch and thread,
shall unfurl the quilt
of the unknown patchwork.

"What is the genius of the craftsman,
but the treasure of the mountain treader?
What is the fool but the learner of wisdom!

"Though numb of faith
in these times of great torment,
doth she not yet cry, the music of lovers,
guarding the womb of the immaculate seed?

"Tales all plentiful,
perplex and scorn,
doth hide in one's cavern,
the tempest of the terrible wrath?

"Doth a force not lie beyond the veil,
unanswered by the bright lance of knowledge?
Full of strangeness are the quiet drifts,
in their transcendental flight of potency.

"Doth not the boundlessness of love share
of the great ocean of dullness and sombreness?

"Dost thou hear the notes
of the saga of the crooked mile,
where struggles the epic climber,
traversing the uncrossable mountain gorge?

"Canst thou feel of the bending,
of the unreachable bough?
Canst thou scent of the unsavoured fruit,
that giveth fragrance
to the voyager of lofty heights?

"Doth yet remain,
the spiritual doorway on its latch?
"Not of strength is the hand
that contemplates its freeing!

Pàl Ó' Siadhail

"Far flung are the petals
of the crimson and honeysuckle,
that kissed the wind
before mutating unto dust,

scattered and spread, all traceless,
the soul of the soil and roots,
forgotten are the unsung
thorns and offshoots,
that once protected the stem.

"Where doth she sway
the sweet secret of pilgrims?
Doth she not dance before thee,
the raven haired gypsy of the caravan?

"Shalt thou not trundle
to the camp of her lasting flame,
and settle by the hearth
of her ancient philosophers?

"For shall taste ye there
the bread of pathfinders,
that celebrates the melting
of the stiffness of lips.

"Shalt thou drink of her wine
crushed of dark forest fruits,
all bursting of juice,
made ripe in summer's bliss?

"Doth listen the lost children
to the ramblings of the nomad,
of barren realms and wasteland?

"What sayeth he, but that empathy becomes
from the battlefield of toil and heartache.

"What sings of he in his joy,
but of the presence of the rushing cascade?
The waterfall of the merriment of tears,
flowing in unfeigned tenderness.

"Is she not torn the heart that catches,
the fall of sweet music?
Dumb is the minstrel to the lasting of strings!

"Doth blow the sorrowful forging
of the blacksmith of dreams,
doth not he ply his mastery
with unforgiving hammer?

"Has been sensed the fright
of poverty and distraction,
or does conditioning prevent
the revealing of lies?

"Where lieth the cracked mirror,
of the reflection of the inescapable truth?
Is already known of her revealing,
with the power to heal sickness?

"Doth hands not desire
the parting of mangled cobwebs
that choke and starve love
in a tightening of consistent drama?

"Doth wish to be protected,
thy wailing and gnashing of fangs?
Or shall be chosen the road
of the impossible journey?

"Where awaits the undertaking
of the emptying of frozen seas,
a frenzied bailing in the face of diligent ice,
scorched by a smelting pitcher of fire.

"Truth unfolds
from the scourge of the relentless labouring,
many are the trials,
each holding of their treasure!

"Wide is the horizon,
where ponders the ancient pine tree,
deep are the roots
dug of intelligent burrowing.

"What speak of, the roots,
but of the mystery of the soil,
what once dreamed of, the sapling,
but of the vastness of the sky.

"Doth not the sprawling of thick forest
behold of the looming of shadows?
Doth not frequent in the leafy foliage,
the shafts of the healing sun?

"For is not the companionship of harmony
encouraging of fruit and playful rhymes?
Silenced is the blacksmith at work,
when the kingdom of birds
converse in their chorus.

"Is unsteadiness not
but the learning of firmness?
Cannot firmness give way
to the strength of the willow?

"Doth not the agile goat
give story to the precipice?
To be bereft of understanding,
is where is witnessed the merging of worlds.

"For not quiet is she yet, the voice,
that shrouds the lonely wayfarer!
Ever encompassing is her ghostly flute,
that giveth cause for contemplation.

"Are they seeping of truth, her echoes,
long known to awaken sleepy eyes?
Doth not ears hear yet,
of the winds of her ceaseless melody?

Pàl Ó' Siadhail

"Doth she not appear before thee,
bearing the weeping of her yearning song?
Doth not streameth her whisper
in the undiluted ocean of quick-silver glass?

"Where but hides in her swaying,
a most perfect and elusive diamond,
carried in the belly of her crystal waves,
where tumbles her torrent
of many unpolished rocks!

"Will be sought for, the priceless jewel,
among the density of the stone laden upsurge,
the untarnished amulet
that offers nought but enlightenment
to the unconscious nature of suppression?

"For parched of thirst is the wasteland
that once gave home to the boundless lake,
sad is the potter who no longer spins
his wheel for the dryness of the clay.

"Of weariness is the observer,
of the pathways of thoughts and daydreams?
Distilled is the vision,
of the seeker void of motion!"

"Shall breath return to the wind of song,
the healer of the trampled spirit,
all broken and sighing?

"For far beyond the gateway
of the tongues of shame and bravery,
is where roams the forger of the master key!

"Not unsolved in the thin realms
is the picking of the unfathomable lock,
not uncharted is the steering
of the mariner in his sightlessness.

"Far flung are the grassy plains
that bear the movement of poetry,
why does the conditioned mind boast then
of freedom and abundance?

"Has parted the eagle from his eyrie,
to lend his call to the leafy forest,
to engage in the sharp conversation,
of the ruggedness of the high peaks?

"Doth swell before thee, the deluge,
that bringeth love to the daunting wilderness?
Canst thou feel of the trundling,
of the majesty of the stag?

"Doth not sleep in the dew
of autumn's retiring,
the secret of summer,
in her withering coat?

"Will remember the children
the fondness of laughter,
the contentment of the seasons,
and the simpleness of the heart?

"Shall not stand again strong,
the Warriors of the Rainbow,
born of the cold lake of crystal?

"For does she not descend,
the ancient chanting,
and the clatter of bossy shields?

"Intelligence of deep canyons,
wrought of stories and sadness,
the unfurling of the soul that shall defy
the drama of the ages.

"For doth not she return, on laden wings,
the turbulent surging of the spiritual cyclone?
Dost thou feel of the muffled murmur of old,
that once rattled the lonely mountain passes?

"Doth eyes weep at the motion
of the long grass in her beauty?
"Or doth the drunkenness of the senses intoxicate,
all making of denial's broken vessel?

"Has fled the traveller from his chains,
beyond the barren realms of captivity?
"Is yet silenced the blacksmith's hammer,
or doth his incantations and embers yet charm?

"For heard is the harp
of the minstrel's mutation,
busy are the fairy women
in their work and gladness.

"Seen are the bluebells,
that chime in distant memory,
scented is the sap of the lofty pine tree
that lends sweet fragrance unto the breeze.

"Do they drop around thee,
the needles of the gnarled pine,
do they lend a strange gentleness
to the storm of unlearning?

"Doth the eddy pull towards thee,
the cycle of confusing currents?
Shall be understood amidst the chaos,
the eloquence of the serenity of the rose?

"Do unclean thoughts deceive
the blossoming of love,
doth the slashing spear of envy
obscure once bright eyes?

"For what indeed is truth,
but the shaper of growth,
what is the resistance to her nature,
but a hindrance to the spring.

"Is remembered the capable spirit
of the undaunted snowdrop,
way-bearer to her brothers and sisters,
not yet revealed in their miracle?

"Where do wings carry the search
of the inquisitive bumble bee?
Where scratch the wretchedness
of stinging claws,
but in a layer constructed of loneliness?

"Doth craft the carpenter his wood,
not knowing of the grain?
Doth forgetfulness dwell
in the memory of the forest?

"Is she ruptured, the vessel,
of the wine-maker's destiny?
"Doth not desire the unsought fruit and herbs,
the mystery of fermentation?

"For who art thou that walketh upon the earth
with breath in thy lungs and strange beholding?
Can be felt of the gypsy's shadow and smile,
dost yet thou lament unto the kingdom of birds?

"Shall tenderness weave her unwoven sail,
hungry for navigation on unvoyaged seas?
"Doth disturb crystal rainfall, the mudded pools,
with the promise of sight and clearness?

"Is not the unstained leaf
but the receiver of intelligent emptiness?
Can she be traced on the heart's shores,
the miraculous shell,
that carries the echo
of the symphony of her waves?

"What would recite the minstrel
without the weeping parables of the traveller?
For what doth pine the traveller,
but for golden song of the minstrel's mastery.

Pàl Ó' Siadhail

"Doth eyes feast upon the chasing of promise,
a sullen beholding for the snaring of joy?
What did happen to the worldly conversation,
once shared by the cave and the horizon?

"Is entangled her art
between the ocean and sky,
more blue than the countless stars,
returning unto oneness?

"For far is the endlessness,
where the horizon resteth,
bottomless is the cave,
where many tunnels twist and meet.

"Are they not desolate and asunder,
the falling feathers of swans,
without the hands that grasp
the understanding in their finding?

"Is not dumbstruck the soothsayer
without the enchanted harp,
that once bellowed eminently
in the pull of his slipstream?

"Dost hear all ye watchers,
over the many great cities,
the song that bore thought into being?

"Dost thou hear of the chiming
of her soundless bell,
calling to pilgrims from her visionless tower?

"Doth she cry, the buttercup,
for the kissing of summer?
Doth dream of the deep slumber of winter,
the pushing of the fauna and flora?

"Can scornful arms be outstretched
across the vastness of fear and wilderness?
Can be clasped the many hands
yet untouched by the medicine of forgiveness?

"Shall oblivious ears comprehend
the silent symphony of strings,
abounding in so many beautiful notes,
that the little birds,
shall never cease in their rhapsody?

"What is the motionless state
that giveth life to the gentle breeze?
"What causeth the roaming of the spirit,
that giveth fervour,
unto the rambler of the savage heath?

"Hidden is the road
of the gypsy's keening,
ever observing is the tongue
that manifests thought.

"Not deceiving is the return
of the typhoon in his powerful blast.
Doth not fright indeed discourage
the continuing of the footsteps of adventure?

"Is she not pathless the soil that beholds
the secret of the seed?
Not hindered is the shape-shifting
cluster of petals
by the determined turning of seasons.

"What is the direction
of the warrior who awakens
from the deep slumber of his sorrowful den?

"What is the cause of his shyness,
that the dreamer should conceal himself
in a labyrinth of solitary worthlessness?

"Not always sharp of sight
recalls the fox of the snowstorms!
For lonely is the wilderness
in the land of unmade trails.

"Terrifying are the shining of eyes
to the wanderer who lost himself.
Sad is the air that never gave his harmony
to the music of the summer breeze.

"For is not life desolate
in the unfolding of learning,
is not faith wrought from the mallet
that crushes and wounds the soul?

"Not agile is the spine
that torments the strength of the seeker,
laden with dense rocks that carry
the weight of a thousand mountains.

"Doth lie a passing
beyond the twisted highway?
Doth peace exist beyond
the horizon of the narrow gap?

"Shall laughter grind away
the chilling of sadness,
or do they dream together
in the awe of the drama?

"Gnarled is the countenance
of the healer of the wild roads,
strong is his chorus
that fractures the veil of numbness.

"Deep is the soul
that faced the Devil and his bargaining,
not slender is the canyon that gushes and boils
in many rapids of strange tales.

"For strong again blow
the winds of the Rainbow Warrior,
not shy are the hearts that carry
the memory of the Great Spirit.

"Not unseen is the Great Mystery
that bore love to the stargazer,
not unheard is the wailing of the children
with the power to heal the mind sickness.

"For not is she mute,
the calling of old,
that frequents the thin and quiet realms.

"Full of thunder is the placidness
of her murmuring
that shakes the heart
of the destitute pilgrim.

"All tossed in ruggedness
is his torrent of tears
that would confuse the ocean's vastness,

felt are the many wanderers
of the terrible trail of thorns,
returning home joyously in the days of prophecy."

Chapter 4

Summary

Wonder resurfaces from the Crystal Lake shaken from the strange experience. Feeling afraid and alone, he begins the long road home where he eventually meets with a scouting party who have been searching for him for some time and who rejoice in his finding. They make the long journey home where a great feast awaits the returning of the child which had already been predicted by the Bear Skin Shaman of the village. With much joy in the air, Wonder is united with his family and his Medicine Wheels, where he begins his musical medley to the delight of the tribe.

Chapter 4

The Road Home

Then quicker than the thrashing
of the honey bee's wings,
did resurface Wonder from deepest waters,
bewildered and all left alone,

for the cold feet of dread and terror
delivered a cutting of icy tidings,
wailing and moaning of how far away
he had travelled from his home.

With his heartbeat racing
like a herd of rampant horses
stampeding their thunder on an open plain,

Wonder left behind him,
the Kingdom of the Crystal Lake,
returning to his distant homeland,
and the tribe from which he came.

Now home to Wonder was known
as the Valley of Sorrow,
where the Devil steers his crooked boat
up and down the River of Weeping.

For it is said
that a sweeping sadness had descended upon
a once green and fruitful valley,
like a thief in the night time, cunning and sly,
while all the tribe were sound in their sleeping.

Retracing his steps
on the trail of the forbidden boundary stone,
great was the weariness
that consumed his strength
with a gnawing of hunger's pain,

when from the belly of the forest
came a wandering cluster of torches,
piercing the black sky's grip
which succumbed to the glowing
and flashing of naked flame.

The echoes full of shouting,
nearer and nearer did come,
thought pondered the question,
of how long had he been gone?

And just like the many tales of adventure,
found in every corner of the world,
Wonder's thoughts unto himself
were indeed to be proved wrong.

The chief tracker,
with hair braided in eagle's feathers,
let shudder his cry,
"It's the boy, it's the boy,
for I cannot believe mine eyes!"

And the truth to this day,
of how long Wonder was gone,
many folk shall tell
that it is not but a pot full
of hocus-pocus and lies.

Wonder and the Medicine Wheels

For seven whole winters
had melted into seven springs,
the scout party had all but yielded defeat,

when the spirit of the forest
released him from her care
'neath the ancient sky,
where the sun, the moon and the stars meet.

"The child is alive, the child is alive!"
joy swirled with a deafening cry,

"Through seven long winters,
we have searched for thee, Wonder,
from the bottomless swamps
to the unreachable peaks on high.

Pàl Ó' Siadhail

"Return home we must
beyond the great forest glade,
many are the miles of trails waiting,
for tired feed grind,

for since thou hast been away,
the tribe has been swollen
with a grief so heavy,
that has taken over thy mother's mind."

The vision of her eyes,
bubbled from deep within Wonder,
the patient Devil stabbed his spear,
full of tormenting emotion,

for on the long journey home,
came a battle with no rest,
a duel between chance and choice,
and their ever draining, chatting, commotion.

Wonder and the Medicine Wheels

For biting indeed was the wound
inflicted from the spear,
the child could not but feel
the pining of his mother's pain,

pain that no words can carry,
for life's puzzles and problems,
hide themselves in many different clouds
of a sad and consuming rain.

A runner from the valley came
to bring the scouting party news,
that the tribe was assembling,
on the Knoll of the Well of Omens,

where being prepared was a mighty feast
'neath the looming eminence
of the great standing stones,
and the scattering of sacred dolmens.

For the Bearskin Shaman
had drunk water from the well
near a smouldering council fire
at the outburst of dawn,

where he saw in his vision quest that morn,
a Rainbow Warrior,
a roving child,
awoken to forgotten song!

"Come let us gather 'midst
the ancient circles of stone!"
shouted the Bearskin Shaman,
full of far-eyed sight.

"Let our bare feet again
walk upon the ancient earth,
let us remember the ways of our ancestors
whoever danced away the night.

Wonder and the Medicine Wheels

"Then we will listen to this adventurer,"
the Bearskin Shaman continued to cry,
"With his stories all told in rhythm and rhyme,

he will impart unto us his tales
of danger and daydreams,
like that of the blind seeker,
who braves the frightful climb,

between a glacier of mystery
drenched and soaked,
with love and fear on either side,

where one false move
can indeed trick the seeker
into a greasy, tumbling, perilous slide.

"But, if his heart is pure,
and the adventurer worthy,
he shall scale the heights
of the slippery tower,

to discover his sight
from the truth of his weeping,
obtaining strength and medicine
from its healing power."

***

With the bulk of the journey
now ground in the dust,
the Knoll of the Well of Omens smiled
and bled her sweet visions,

where the waxing harvest moon
blew light on the horizon,
the birthing stars winked in their bliss
in the high realms of the puzzling heavens.

Wonder and the Medicine Wheels

The breath of freedom leaned
to the roving north wind,
wild and unbound like the rebel's tongue

that knows no sound but its native ways,
a heathen spirit driven wildly
with an earthly hum.

The giant drummer thumped
his instrument of deer hide,
the rousing fiddler swished
his playful jig,

while the heartfelt piper kissed
the lips of the strumming harper,
bright was the musical sound,
of the ascending shindig.

Pàl Ó' Siadhail

The scouting party reached
the ceremonial entrance,
through the great row of obelisks
that led toward the curious circle of stone,

where the primal roar emerged,
engulfing the tribe.
Wonder, the pathfinder of dreams,
it seemed, had at long last, returned back home.

***

Embracing his mother,
his father and sister,
who went by the name
of the Buttercup Maiden,

a girl with hair woven from a blaze
of countless golden sun drops,
with a fiery heart as red as the rowan berry
that ripens at summer's fading.

The gossip not shy of loose lips
bustled through the feast,
conjuring many tales
of the strange matter at hand,

while the band rocked and rolled
its shaking of soul,
which carried its echo unto the rainbow's end
in a far off untroubled land.

The mystic archer skipped and spun
to the honey-drenched harmony,
before stretching the stardust string
of his glistening spirit bow,

aiming a raft of cheerful arrows
at the shadows of tears,
which stained the once green valley,
so dear to the tribe's bruised heart and soul.

Pàl Ó' Siadhail

Then did crash the Bearskin Shaman,
"Silence!"
with his staff carved ingeniously
from a twisted branch of indigenous pine.

A wooden rod notched in symbols
and archaic writ,
which preserved great mysteries
and cryptic cipher,
etched thoughtfully in unbroken line.

Bold was the form of wild garb
and talismans of the medicine man,
elevated in his clairvoyant sight
from the top of the sacred mound,

the thin place between
the noble megaliths of awe,
a perfect monument expertly raised upon
an old and hallowed ground.

The little birds of the twilight
whistled their wondrous chorus
to the rooted beating
of Earth Mother's spellbinding drum.

The swollen horizon's uproar
trickled into the west,
boasting proudly before fleeing,
with its capture, the sun.

Then did disappear the colourful mirage,
retiring unto her sleeping,
the lonesome rider of the darkness,
let whip his stead of the night,

for had come creeping in his noiselessness,
the fateful hour,
for Wonder to spin his musical medley,
spitting zealous chants
of the children's healing plight.

Now on top of the fabled fairy knoll
lay the Medicine Wheels,
which ached of raw pain and the longing
for his master's return,

where once again in imagination,
and her realms of light wings,
they would blend earthen drones
and perceptive verses
with a deep digging soul that burned.

"Hello my dearest of brothers,
has not passed a while?"
said Wonder fondly,
to his beloved Medicine Wheels.

"For seven years I did travel,
all high and low,
lost in the land of the forgotten tribes,
where glow the many golden fairy fields.

"So let's roll the fathomless tempo
hit from Earth Mother's drum,
and let fly unchained creation's force,
and her threads of unshakable love,

Where honour we shall,
the dance of our forebears,
who once churned the soil
'neath the laughing of stars above."

The domain of the night sky,
stretched in her endlessness and vastness,
old grandmother owl of the tree tops circled
in her hunting and drifting soar,

hooting her wisdom to the bend
of aged Destiny's call,
for the strange dancing to begin
its curing twist on the floor.

Pàl Ó' Siadhail

The tribe stood hypnotized,
awaiting Wonder's unveiling of dreams,
who himself stood, rather nervously,
in the centre of the sacred mound.

From the ether roared the memory
of the beautiful mermaid and the Crystal Lake,
lamenting of weighty teachings,
calling for Earth Mother's drums to pound.

***

So Wonder began
his spinning, whirling medley
in the loose motion of a deluge
of many rolling and tumbling stones,

stones that gathered no moss
until they splashed with muddy waters
where the heavy-hearted catfish
tunefully gurgles and groans.

The Bearskin Shaman
let his backbone slip,
to the spine tingling concoction
of drums, strings and wailing harp,

the howling white wolf in the distance,
moaned an untamed key of approval,
the tribe paused from the thrill
and ferocious dancing,
in order to give cheer and clap.

The native dance of kicking heels
spread wildly throughout the shindig,
while the pondering child
sparked the wheels alight.

For what was to burst from within
the crackling of fire,
was the unstained vision,
of a daydreamer's far-seeing sight.

"With deep breath at hand!"
Wonder yelled to the Horn of Echoes,
It's time for the workings of the poet,
unbound in his kind,

let's muster a most rare rhyme
and give life to the story,
of the perplexing journey
of the road of the heart,
where lies one's own hidden
treasure to find!"

Chapter 5

Summary

To the backbeat of earthen drums, Wonder delivers some of his newly discovered philosophy with his Horn of Echoes that projects his voice over the music. The music and rhyming continue through the night, when eventually tiredness kicks in and the tribe return home to their beds. The Bear Skin Shaman remains awake through the birth of daylight, brewing a potion and reciting incantations and lore at his cauldron to which the animals of the forest hearken.

Chapter 5

Wonder's Tune

Pàl Ó' Siadhail

"Bursting like the rocky canyon
of the endless search,
awoken has the spirit to the surge
of dream tracker's thrust,

not of rest is the voice, but loud,
like the legend of fire mountain
that shudders in his whisper,
lying waiting to erupt.

"Bright is the catapult forged in youth,
strapped over broader shoulders,
packed in full is the earthen pouch
of many pebbles quarried of love,

sharp of the slingshot's aiming,
with gems blustering towards the heart
is what sighs of the dreaming pilgrim,
'neath the rock-laden clouds above!

Wonder and the Medicine Wheels

"Imaging the path laid before,
through every changing season,
reminding are the omens,
every draw of breath is for a reason,

wandered through the snow of cruel winters,
melting,
great frozen lakes on the way,

terrible is the journey,
that passes through the underworld,
known to lead even the most
perceptive of travellers astray.

"For is not life
but a heavenly flower,
full of stirring and promise
within her seed?

Where if one can brave bad weather
until the sun rises,
will not be discovered a chance indeed?

"For summer she will unfurl
with her silver moon fall,
where wisdom blows his most ancient tune,

for all the heavenly flowers
of wonder and awe,
whose time has come to rise and bloom!

"The breath is a reminder of a slow
and superstitious departing,
cannot dreams be then
but a calling to adventure,
a blind quest perhaps worth starting?

"Golden sunbeams will follow
the endless pouring of poison rainfall
'neath a blue sky so pure,
of the sprawling vastness
that it was sprung from.

"An understanding lieth there,
no rambling of thoughts
will ever convey,

not wise is the tongue
of the Devil's sarcasm,
nor loving his attentive eyes that prey.

"Not forgotten is the medicine
scented in loneliness,
for born there is the action
of the master hunter,

he who knows of pathways
cultivated from ice storms
and a smashing of the heart,
all broken and asunder.

"For is not life
but a heavenly flower,
full of stirring and promise
within her seed?

Where if one can brave bad weather
until the sun rises,
will not be discovered a chance indeed?

"For summer she will unfurl
with her silver moon fall,
where wisdom blows his most ancient tune

for all the heavenly flowers
of wonder and awe,
whose time has come to rise and bloom!

"The Great Spirit that dwelleth
in every living thing,
commands the pendulum's sway,

for all the children to observe
Earth Mother and learn,
of her beautiful and forgotten ways,

believed in, with much force of being,
is the truth of prophecy's fabulous sight,

aware of the frightening occurrences
and sad depressions,
that every Rainbow Warrior has to fight.

"For the true labyrinth
of bewildering treasure
is to dig for one's own soul,

like the labouring badger
that burrows a home
so his cubs may flourish and grow.

"An opening lies deep within
the innermost realms,
where the silent piper doth sweetly drone.

Begging to be followed,
is the grace of his wandering,
captivated by the air of his enchanted tones.

"For is not life
but a heavenly flower,
full of stirring and promise,
within her seed?

Where if one can brave bad weather
until the sun rises,
will not be discovered a chance indeed?

"For summer she will unfurl
with her silver moon fall,
where wisdom blows his most ancient tune

for all the heavenly flowers
of wonder and awe,
whose time has come to rise and bloom!"

***

So, with a dip dap dapping,
and a rip rap rapping,
and a clip clap snappity doo,

versed the rhymer with his horn,
until the snoozing morn was born
from the veiled land of the east
swabbed in a dripping of colour,
of yellows, reds and blues.

Well did not laughter and merriment
wisp into passing,
without mention of his encounter
with the beautiful mermaid said.

For Wonder feared
that unto most people's ears,
that the tale would sound as if he was
not at all quite sane in the head.

So the gathering dispersed
toward their earthen abodes,
much was the exhaustion from the rigour
of the heel shaking fury,

settling down by the hearth
all safe and snug,
tucked up in their bed
with their dreams securely.

And while the tribe did drift away,
to the hush-a-bye baby
fast asleep on lullaby's ocean,

one remained awakened
through the birth of daylight,
mumbling and fumbling
'bout a bygone, ancient potion.

For frequenting the sacred spot
by the Well of Omens,
the Bearskin Shaman at his cauldron
did vigorously stir,

chanting out strongly
incantations and lore,
raising the ghosts of the spirit world
into a spiralling whir.

"Hubble bubble, I see,
a lost love amidst the trouble,
shining is the solitary star
that braves the night time's sky,

for it seems the sanctuary
of the tender poet's sweet repose,
has stirred from the ether once more,
in his heartfelt cry.

Pàl Ó' Siadhail

"A maker of tales, a crafter of rhyme,
plucked from the great lake
of the Creator's pondering,

that shall unleash visions
of courage and daydreams,
where many seekers shall again succumb
to the call of the mystic wandering.

"A mystery, great wizardry,
sorcery wrapped in antiquity
of the storyteller, a forest dweller,
a lonely fellow, versed in secret history.

"For is returning the day
when the children will play,
where no one can scold their imagination.

"For within this quiet vision
there lies a decision
to change our direction
towards a new vibration!"

Wonder and the Medicine Wheels

The tumbling chorus
of the early morning birds,
warmly praised the sun
in his ascending dance,

for so joyful was their music,
to the ears of the Bearskin Shaman
that he stomped in great vigour,
before he fell into trance.

Bawling out chants that carried
far beyond the tombstones,
where lay in their legend
the mighty giants of renown,

"Twist in your graves,
venerable bones of lost kings,
let loose the hounds of the Rainbow Warriors,
who have returned to claim their crown!"

Pàl Ó' Siadhail

Far did travel the fervour
of the storming of music,
sharp was the hearing of the forest creatures
to the blast of a messenger of yore,

that would whip up the winds of dreams,
long foretold in the slipstream of oracles,
of the teachings of nature
which sacred Earth Mother
so tenderly and lovingly bore.

"Sing the song of old, beloved Earth Mother,
not forgotten is the land of milk and honey,
drench the valleys and high peaks
in shapeless loving,
bending free and fair,

purifying are the remedies
that dwell among
the creatures of wild heath and forest,
healers of the mind sickness
that burdens the soul's yearning,
weighing all a-heavy, in a haunting despair!"

Chapter 6

Summary

The Bearskin Shaman praises Earth Mother and the forgotten healing remedies of the forest animals in heartfelt cry.

Chapter 6

Medicine

Pàl Ó' Siadhail

"Let rut and roar fiercely,
shaggy coated king of stags,
shake the antlers in fury
that twist and grace
the loftiness of rocky peaks.

"Spring and bound in your glory
across the deluge of boggy marshland,
impart the wisdom of the elements' rasp,
that mutates encroaching danger
into a sunny and tranquil peace.

"Thrash enthusiastic wings like lightning,
most intelligent darting bumble bee,
buzz among the many colourful flowers
that bear such beauty in their petals.

"Enrich the land with the joy of flight
and busy tales of delicious honey,
build industriously great hives,
protected in swarm,
where no impostor dare ever meddle.

"Pierce and burst from the depths
of the fertile soil,
O courageous badger of the scraping hooks,
tell the healing stories, full of burrowing,
and the constructing of tunnels deep,

scratched and crafted in persistence,
in the light of a blind struggle through darkness,
for always were ye known as brave,
and as a creator of kingdoms
that frequent the earthen, realms beneath.

"Come out from thy den,
all growling and snarling,
dear secretive nimble mountain lion,
jumper of the high cliffs that tumble unto,
the many bounteous valleys and oaken groves,

where the soothsayer of old
would cry and pine
of the nobility of the skilful hunt,
for only of awe is the stillness,
and patience that trusts,
intuition, and its expert flow.

Pàl Ó' Siadhail

"Spin in the dirt and disperse
the itching of flies,
O snorting boar of the sharp tusks,
for would she not indeed be sad,
the abundant forest,
without the patter of unflinching hooves,

hooves that scuttle around in prosperity,
defying the cunning of the predator,
where fearlessness grunts
at the stalking of terror,
that shall smell timidity
before any gnashing chase pursues.

"Whistle and warble proudly,
O chirping red robin of the bushy thicket,
for tenacious is thy melody,
which battles gallantly
the unceasing winter's blanket of snow,

bright is the pecking that scavenges
and feasts upon
the many insects and earthen worms,
hardy are the wings that flit,
amidst the brambles and thorns,
entangling of shrubs, and their craving to grow.

"Trundle the trails with weighty paws,
great bear who watches and guards the world,
wade in thy sovereignty the rushing cascade
that carries the salmon of many leaps.

Hearty is the roar of willpower's surging,
that laughs at intimidation with goading face,
legendary are the claws
wrought of trampling and slashing,
thick is the skin, where no cold ever seeps.

"Splash the tail that eludes the current's force,
dear determined and earnest brother beaver,
overseer of nature's order and harmony,
clever builder of lodges and protective dams,

for were not always barriers erected by fear,
that cut off love as a threatening enemy,
for inventive are the walls
of the architect tree feller,
protecting the balance of the thriving wetlands.

"Wail and moan, with lungs full of breath,
howling white wolf of the coat
of a hundred thousand winters,
long have you studied
the waxing and waning of the moon,
learning the language of loyalty and success,

for safe is the pack of the sprightly cubs,
that encourages the sense of the finest chieftain,
who leads from the front, bold and bare-toothed
at the trespassing of foes
seeking to disrupt and distress.

"Sing of the chrysalis, of the mysterious process,
most graceful skipping butterfly,
of magic is the mutation
that transforms the crawl
of a caterpillar's munching quest,

that will accept an unknown change,
undeterred by the darkness,
not clinging to dreams of a leafy joy,
is not the emptying of desire
but a quickening of wits,
where the unfolding of bright wings
are made manifest?

"Spread widely, the robust wings
that once circled the sun,
O mighty and soaring golden eagle,
revealer of the Great Spirit's heavenly creations,
that observes all in sacred manner,
with keen sense.

For is it not of wonder, the grasping of talons,
is it not of awe, the call of the powerful beak,
is it not of artistry, the twigs that weave the eyrie,
a potent medicine to widen
the narrowness of minds,
ridding of opinion and rigidness
in purifying cleanse.

"So sing the song of old, beloved Earth Mother,
not forgotten is the land of milk and honey,
drench the valleys and high peaks
in shapeless loving,
bending free and fair,

purging are the remedies
that dwell among
the creatures of the wild heath and forests,
healers of the mind sickness
that burdens the soul's yearning,
weighing all a-heavy, in a haunting despair!"

Chapter 7

Summary

After sleeping in their beds until the mid-part of the day, the tribe is awoken by the barking of hunting hounds. The village springs to life only to find that another adventure is unfolding...

Chapter 7

The Untamed Wind

Pàl Ó' Siadhail

So the following morning did bid
a warm and cheerful goodbye,
fading into the strange frontier,
vanishingly broadly
between the earth and sky.

A feisty red rooster,
around the village strutted around,
crowing a cockle doodle daisy,
while the midday sun did scorch the ground.

A pair of snoozing hunting hounds,
from deep slumber did blink
their awakening eyes,
shaking and itching their ruffled coats,
dispersing the cluster
of many bloodthirsty flies.

Wonder and the Medicine Wheels

When the feast of scratching
reached its climax,
satisfied tails began
to vigorously let waggle,

from great sturdy heads
and long droopy mouths
tough jaws of dripping spit
let bark a yip yapping prattle,

in a seamless flight of the language
of the canine breed,
the dogs revived the tribe
from the far-off realms of sleep.

Many a yawning man and woman arose
to the rumble of hunger's plea,
while recalling the gathering's dancing fervour
and their thoughts of feeling free.

Pàl Ó' Siadhail

Waves of fresh cooked bread
and the fragrance of salted butter
spread tastily from home to home.

But where was Wonder?
his Mother loudly cried,
for already up away and gone
was the distant child,
like the restless wind on a ceaseless roam.

***

Now poets will rant
and the melody of birds chirp and cheep
of enchanted dew drops
and bursting seeds,

of mystical mountain passes
all heavenly winding,
hidden jewels of wisdom
and the journey in their finding.

Wonder and the Medicine Wheels

Where Wonder now rambles,
well, nobody knows,
some say that he dwells
in the shadows and darkness,
where a smouldering light yet glows.

Others speak of unearthly voices
that faintly whisper upon the restless breeze,
which descends upon the fruitful forests,
rustling among the majesty of virgin trees.

Oral traditions and legends
speak of silent pipes
adrift on the slipstream
of creaking silver galleys,

a magical searching,
on the lost ocean of blind mariners,
far, far beyond the land
of green leafy valleys.

Pàl Ó' Siadhail

But if fortunate thou art dear listener
of sensitive hearing,
to stumble on a place
filled with rugged oak and pine,

And if hear ye will there
the murmur of the babbling brook,
be sure to let thy mind roam
like the trickling flow
that meanders, twists and winds.

For she will carry thee away
on the bright wings of daydreams,
and there in thy flight may be sensed
the fragrance of the Kingdom of the Crystal Lake,

where hiding among the thick growth
on the faraway shore,
lies a most peculiar and mysterious gateway,
where the Rainbow Warrior awaits,
beyond the threshold,
to tempt one's consciousness, to stir, and wake...

39070206R00092

Printed in Poland
by Amazon Fulfillment
Poland Sp. z o.o., Wrocław